Running
Behind

Running Behind

Sylvia Taekema

ORCA BOOK PUBLISHERS

Library and Archives Canada Cataloguing in Publication

Taekema, Sylvia, 1964–, author
Running behind / Sylvia Taekema.
(Orca currents)

Issued in print and electronic formats.
ISBN 978-1-4598-1798-2 (softcover).—ISBN 978-1-4598-1799-9 (PDF).—
ISBN 978-1-4598-1800-2 (EPUB)

I. Title. II. Series: Orca currents
PS8639.A25R86 2018   jC813'.6   C2017-907680-9
                            C2017-907681-7

First published in the United States, 2018
Library of Congress Control Number: 2018933734

Summary: In this high-interest novel for middle readers, Jake can't
wait to compete in the upcoming cross-country championships.
A free teacher guide for this title is available at orcabook.com.

MIX
Paper from
responsible sources
FSC® C016245
www.fsc.org

*Orca Book Publishers is dedicated to preserving the environment and has
printed this book on Forest Stewardship Council® certified paper.*

Orca Book Publishers gratefully acknowledges the support
for its publishing programs provided by the following agencies:
the Government of Canada through the Canada Book Fund and the
Canada Council for the Arts, and the Province of British Columbia
through the BC Arts Council and the Book Publishing Tax Credit.

Cover photography by Unsplash.com/Anton Darius Sollers
Author photo by Trish Wolting-Meiboom

ORCA BOOK PUBLISHERS
orcabook.com

Printed and bound in Canada.

21 20 19 18 • 4 3 2 1

For Steven: great runner, great friend, just the kind of guy you want to have at your back

Chapter One

The whistle blew, signaling the end of the sprints. The boys gathered around their coach. "Well," he said, lifting his Diamonds cap and resettling it a little farther back on his head, "what do you think? You ready, Jake?"

Jake rolled his shoulders. "Ready, Coach."

"Sure?"

"One hundred percent."

"Shawn?"

Shawn pulled off the headband holding back his long, wavy hair and gave Coach Dave a thumbs-up. "Ready, Coach."

"Don't grow any taller in the next few days or you're going to lose a lot of time ducking under every tree branch on that course."

"Yessir! I mean, no, sir. No growing."

"Ready, Tony?"

Tony was rooting around in the bottom of the backpack he'd pulled off the picnic table. He held a flattened granola bar in one hand. "Ready, Coach."

"You going to pack that bag full of snacks for the trip?"

"I was thinking I might need a bigger one."

Coach Dave chuckled. "You could be right. Ready, Sam?"

Sam nodded. "Ready, Coach."

"No projects planned? No assignments due?"

"My schedule is clear for takeoff."

"Right. Ready, Spencer?"

"Always ready to run."

"Good. We're going to miss Paul, but we're glad to have you on board." Finally, Coach Dave turned to look at the boy beside him. "So, Simon, think this bunch is ready?"

Jake watched Simon push up his glasses and look around the circle of sweaty boys gathered in the parking lot. They had just finished their final cross-country practice before the provincial race in Barry's Bay. Simon locked eyes with Jake and grinned. "It's a dream team, best I've seen, hot as lava, cool as ice cream."

Coach Dave laughed. "Good to know you're ready too, Mr. Assistant Coach. Well, that's it then. We'll see you Friday morning. Eat well, sleep well, pack light." As the boys started to gather their stuff, he continued. "Don't forget your team jerseys. You guys are the regional silver medalists. You're going to the provincials. You have earned this opportunity through dedication, determination, talent and hard work. Do your region proud. Do your team proud. Do yourselves proud."

Shawn wiped an imaginary tear from his cheek. "That was beautiful, Coach."

The coach smiled. "Now get out of here."

Sam high-fived his teammates and started walking home. Spencer and Simon jogged to the bus stop. Shawn and Tony headed to the variety store across the road. Jake went to unlock his bike.

"What do you think, Jake?" asked Coach Dave.

"About what?"

"The team, the weekend, the race."

Jake closed his eyes. The race was all he'd been thinking about since the moment they found out they'd qualified. His whole body felt like it was buzzing. "It's going to be awesome. I can't wait."

"Me neither," said the coach.

"Tony's got so much power, and Shawn can cover a lot of ground with those long legs of his. Sam's so speedy and so smart about how he runs a race, and Spencer, he's just so smooth. He runs so easily. So fast. No worries or hangups. It's like nothing can throw him off."

"He loves to run, that's for sure. But don't downplay your own part in this, Jake. If I know you, you'll find your way up front. I've got to admit, I like our chances. You guys have got heart. Plus, we've got a secret weapon."

"We do?"

"Simon's jokes!" Coach Dave high-fived Jake and got into his van.

"Whatever happens this weekend, it's sure going to be something to remember. You okay to get home?"

Jake nodded.

"Still biking, huh? Might as well while you still can." The coach tugged the zipper on his jacket up a little higher and scanned the sky. "One of these days it's going to snow."

Chapter Two

Jake took one last look at the picture on the screen and then shut down the computer. He'd been looking at photos of the Barry's Bay area. Lakes, hills, trees. It looked awesome. Jake was tired, but he didn't know if he'd be able to sleep. Excited didn't even come close to describing how he felt.

So much had been going on lately. There was the big cross-country run in Deep Rapids the previous Saturday, where the Diamonds had come in second overall. Jake glanced at the silver medal hanging over the corner of his bulletin board and grinned. Then came the news that the team had qualified for the provincial race this weekend in Barry's Bay. And then the final city race just the day before, where Spencer had come in first and Jake, right on his heels, was a close second. He could still hear the cheers and feel the sting of the high fives from his friends on the team.

Coach Dave had told them that their other regular teammate, Paul, had come down with chicken pox and wouldn't be able to make it to Barry's Bay. Jake had recommended inviting Spencer to run in Paul's place, surprising even himself.

All season long he'd considered Spencer Solomon his enemy number one. But that was only because Spencer had come in first in every city race he'd run—races that Jake had been trying so hard, sometimes too hard, to win. But there was no denying that Spencer was one amazing runner. Now they'd be teammates, and Jake couldn't be happier.

Jake placed his team jersey in the duffel bag. He'd finish packing the next day, but he didn't want to risk forgetting his jersey. He was glad Spencer had been able to come out to practice on such short notice and that their buddy Simon was there as well. Simon was a good guy, and he was funny. He'd come all the way to Deep Rapids just to cheer Jake on and had instantly made friends with the rest of the team. So Coach Dave had invited him to Barry's Bay. His main duty was to provide encouragement and comic relief for the team.

When Jake had become obsessed with winning that autumn, it was Simon who had pointed out it was doing him more harm than good. Coach Dave had told him just to run because he loved it. At practice this afternoon Jake had caught himself being a little too hard on the other guys. He just wanted to make sure they were taking the race seriously. This was a big chance for them, and he knew they could do well. Coach Dave had given him a wink when he saw Jake deliberately backing off. They were already a good team. They all knew what they needed to do out there. Jake knew they could count on every team member to do his job. No need to worry.

As he got ready to climb into bed, Jake heard the doorbell. He glanced at his clock. Ten o'clock. Pretty late for visitors. It was probably one of Luke's friends coming to pick him up so they could go out to listen to a band somewhere. Jake's brother Luke was a musician. He had a big concert coming up in a couple of weeks. By then the big race would already be history. Jake's eyes traveled once more to the silver medal hanging above his desk. Was it crazy to think they might earn another one? He smiled. They sure could try.

Jake lay back on his bed, hands behind his head. He took in a deep breath and then let it out slowly. He had just closed his eyes when he heard a soft knock on his door.

"Jake?"

He sat up again quickly. "Yeah?"

His mother opened the door. "I thought you'd still be awake." She smiled. "Listen, your coach is here.

He's wondering if he can talk to you for a minute."

"Coach Dave? Why?"

"He didn't say. Why don't you come find out?"

Chapter Three

Jake pulled a sweatshirt over his pajamas and hurried downstairs to the kitchen. What news couldn't wait until the team loaded up the van Friday morning? Jake didn't know if he could take any more. He was going to go into excitement overload.

His parents sat at either end of the table. Jake slid into the seat across from Coach Dave. Uh-oh. Something was up. The coach wasn't a big man, but he looked like he'd shrunk somehow since Jake had seen him last, just hours earlier. He still had his coat on, and he slumped on the chair. His Diamonds hat sat on the table in front of him, and his hair was messy. Jake figured he knew what this was all about. The coach was worried that Jake was so focused on winning again that he wouldn't run his best or treat his teammates and competitors right. Those couple of slips at practice today were probably still bothering him, and he wanted to talk to Jake about them. Make sure he was on track. Run to run, was Coach Dave's philosophy. Winning will take care of itself. Well, Jake would set his mind at ease. There was no problem.

"Jake—" Coach Dave began.

Jake jumped right in. "Coach, I know I was a little tense at practice today, but I feel good. I feel loose. I won't get a case of the worrywarts. Promise. Chicken pox is enough to deal with, right?" He laughed.

The coach smiled weakly. "Right. That's great, but I'm afraid I have some bad news." He ran his hand over his face.

"What news?"

"It's Spencer."

"Spencer?"

"He called me about an hour ago. He says…he says he can't run this weekend."

What? This was the last thing Jake had expected to hear. He felt his heart begin to beat faster, and his face got hot. "What do you mean? He said he was coming. He was super pumped about it. What happened?"

"He didn't explain. Just said he was sorry, but he couldn't come."

"Sorry? It's Wednesday night. We leave Friday morning. That's awfully short notice."

"Well, to be fair, we didn't give him much notice either, did we, Jake? We only asked him yesterday. Maybe he forgot he had something else planned."

"Then he shouldn't have agreed so quickly. Or he should realize that this race is more important than whatever it is he is doing. Way more important."

"Jake, listen, I was able to put Spencer's name in because he's already listed as a runner in the city league, but—"

"Never mind Spencer then." Jake waved his hand in the air. "Choose another name off the list. Maybe Max Chen can come. He's a good runner."

"No, it's too late. He's not—"

"Or Simon. He's been out with us already. He was at practice today.

He knows the game plan." Jake felt a dull throbbing in his temples. Simon wasn't very fast, he thought to himself, but maybe…

Dave was shaking his head. "Jake, you don't understand. I already filed the entrance papers online. We're registered. You, Sam, Tony, Shawn, Spencer. That's our team. I was able to substitute Spencer in for Paul, but I can't change any of those five names now."

Jake swallowed hard. "You can't change the names?"

"No."

"Did you tell Spencer that?"

"Yes."

"That means *none* of us can go?"

Dave sighed. "I'm afraid it looks that way."

The only sound in the kitchen was the steady ticking of the clock. After a long moment Jake asked, "Did you tell the other guys?"

"Not yet." Dave looked at his watch and sighed again. "I wanted to tell each of you in person. Your house was closest. But I think it's too late now to tell the others tonight. I'll let them know tomorrow."

No one said anything for a few minutes. Finally Dave pushed back his chair. He cleared his throat and picked up his hat. He shook hands with Jake's parents. "Seems a shame," said Jake's dad, shaking his head.

Jake stuffed his bare feet into his sneakers and walked Dave to his van. It was cold outside, but they didn't hurry.

"Jake," said Dave, "I know you're disappointed. I am too. I just can't tell you how sorry I am about this."

There was that word again. Dave was sorry. Spencer was sorry. Somehow sorry just didn't cut it. The anger Jake felt began to warm him up.

This wasn't right. He was going to go and talk with Spencer.

"There's got to be a way we can fix this," said Jake, rubbing his hands up and down his arms. "I have an idea. Could you hold off just a bit on telling the guys?"

"Sure, but I've turned it over and over in my head, Jake. I've even talked to the race organizers. I don't think there's anything we can do."

Jake nodded. "You're probably right. But I'll give you a call in the morning. Don't do anything until then. Please?"

Chapter Four

Jake didn't sleep much. He got up way before his alarm went off and almost tripped on the duffel bag lying open on the floor. Would he still need it this weekend? He pulled on some sweats and made his way downstairs. The dark was just dissolving into gray. He scribbled a quick note with his running route so his parents wouldn't worry and slipped outside.

The frosty air stung a little when Jake sat down on the cold, concrete step to pull on his shoes. He double knotted the laces and tugged on his hat. He felt awful, not just for himself, but for the whole team. He was the one who had insisted Dave ask Spencer to join them in the first place. He should have left well enough alone. Jake wanted to blast Spencer for being so selfish. What could be more important than going to this race? It was the *provincials*. This was a big deal. Or maybe it didn't matter to a hotshot runner like Spencer. Maybe he did that kind of thing all the time.

After some stretches, Jake blew into his hands, shook them out and began the jog over to Spencer's house. It was pretty far, but that was okay. Jake needed time to settle down and work out what he was going to say. He couldn't show up at someone's house so early the streetlights were still on and pretend he was just making a friendly visit. Spencer would know exactly why he'd come.

Before he knew it Jake had turned the last corner. Spencer's house was the third one in. Simon's was the fourth. Several cars were still parked along the street, and few people were out and about yet. He hoped he wasn't too early. Determined to get the weekend back on course, Jake pushed open the gate and made his way up the path to the porch. Then he stood there, staring down at the flagstones, trying to figure out how to begin.

"Hey."

Jake almost jumped out of his skin. Spencer was sitting on the porch steps untying his shoes. He'd been out for a run too.

Spencer looked at him, then down at his shoes again. "You heard from Dave."

"Yeah. Last night."

Spencer nodded but didn't say anything.

"What's up?"

"I, uh, I've got something else this weekend."

"You can't get out of it?"

"I can't get out of it."

"You know this means none of us can go." Jake tried to keep his voice even, but it was hard.

Spencer looked his way again. "I'm sorry," he said, shaking his head. "I can't help it."

Jake's hands balled into fists. He tried hard not to yell. "Of course you can help it. Look, we can fix this," he said evenly.

"No."

"I'm sure if—"

"No."

Jake was becoming frustrated. "Won't you even try to work with me here? Maybe running doesn't mean as much to you, but the rest of the guys worked really hard and were really looking forward to—"

Spencer stood up quickly. "Stop."

Jake stopped. There was something strange in Spencer's voice.

"Running does mean a lot to me. It does. I really want to go with you, but I can't."

Jake took a deep breath. "Okay. Well, you'd better explain, or we're all just going to think you're a jerk."

"You don't understand."

"You're right, I don't. So make me. What's so important this weekend?"

Spencer sat down again but didn't answer.

"I'm not leaving until I know," said Jake firmly.

Spencer shrugged. "I'm spending the weekend with my dad."

"What, he doesn't live with you? I get that. That happens, and it's lousy, but can't you reschedule? Come on, man. It's the provincials. We need you!"

Something banged against the door. Spencer got up quietly and opened it. A man rolled out in a wheelchair.

"Thanks, Spence, but I could have gotten the door. Are you coming in? Breakfast's almost ready." He looked over at Jake and smiled. "Good morning."

"Dad, this is Jake."

Jake nodded. "Hi."

"Nice to meet you, Jake. So you're a runner too," he said, looking down at Jake's shoes. "Did you guys just go out for a jog together?"

Jake started to reply, but Spencer's dad continued on. "It's nice to have a running partner. I told Spencer he should look into joining a team."

Jake looked puzzled. Spencer jumped in quickly. "Dad, we're just going to do a quick cooldown. Back in fifteen, okay?"

"Okay," said Spencer's dad. "But no more than that. You don't want to miss out on my famous pancakes." He spun his chair and went back into the house.

Chapter Five

Spencer pulled Jake out of the yard and started running down the sidewalk.

Jake hurried to keep up. "Spencer, wait. That's your dad? Then he *does* live with you. But I thought I saw you with your family a while ago, at the new pizza place, and he…"

Spencer kept running. "He what? Wasn't in a wheelchair?" He shook his head. "That was my uncle Jerry. He took me and my mom and my sister out for pizza. My dad was in the hospital overnight for some tests."

"Okay, but what gives? Your dad doesn't even know anything about the Diamonds club or about this race. If you tell him, I'm sure—"

Spencer stopped and leaned up against a lamppost. He suddenly seemed very tired. "It's complicated."

"Try me, or I'm going back to your house to eat your pancakes and ask your dad what's going on."

"My sister has a gymnastics competition in Hamilton this weekend. My mom's going with her. It's been planned for weeks, but of course I didn't pay much attention to the dates and stuff."

"Okay."

"They're taking the car."

"And?"

"So I can't go."

"Why?"

"Because my mom is taking the car."

"Why does that matter? We're all going up to Barry's Bay in Dave's van. There's just enough room for all seven of us."

"Exactly. I can't go if my dad doesn't go."

"But it's okay if none of us can go?"

Spencer frowned but didn't reply.

"Can't we just go explain things to your parents and work something out?"

"No! Listen, as soon as I heard about my sister's plans for the weekend, I didn't even tell my mom and dad about the race. There's no point."

"But how do you know you can't go if you didn't even ask? Come on, let's find out."

"No. It's a Saturday. I have to be with my dad."

Jake looked at Spencer. There was more to this, he could tell. "Why are you doing this to the team?"

"Look, Jake, I don't know you very well. Maybe I should tell you the whole story, but I don't know if I can trust you to keep it to yourself."

"You can. I promise."

Spencer sighed. He swiped at his eyes. "Cold air always makes my eyes water," he mumbled.

Jake knew it wasn't the cold air. "Yeah," he said, "mine too."

Spencer cleared his throat. "My dad was in a car accident at the end of January. It was really snowy, and he got T-boned by another driver. His back is messed up. He can't work. We all hoped that he would recover completely, but the tests he just had showed that's probably not going to happen."

Jake paused before he answered. He knew he had to be careful. "That's rough, Spencer. I'm really sorry, but..." He paused and took a deep breath. He needed to finish this. "I still don't understand what that has to do with the race this weekend."

Spencer didn't look up from the sidewalk as he spoke. "It's my fault. It was Saturday, and I was supposed to go with him. I had something else I wanted to do instead. I can't even remember what it was anymore. Something unimportant. And he got hurt. I should have been there."

"Spencer, think. If you had been there you might have been hurt too—or worse."

"No, don't you see? I might have been able to see the other guy coming. I might have been able to warn my dad. If I'd been there, maybe the accident wouldn't have happened at all. We would have stopped for donuts or something and he wouldn't even have been in the wrong place at the wrong time. He always liked to get donuts when we were out together."

"But that doesn't make sense. You're not responsible for what happened."

"Maybe not. But I know one thing. We do Saturdays together. If my dad can't come to the race, I'm not racing."

"But you love to run."

"I do. I used to run with my dad. Sometimes I feel guilty for still running when he can't, but it makes me feel so… free." He shook his head. "But I'm not running this weekend."

Jake wanted to argue, but he understood the pain he saw on Spencer's face. He sighed and began to walk away.

"Jake, you said I could trust you. You won't tell anyone, will you? You can't. Especially my dad. He would make me go."

"I want him to make you go."

"I know. But it's no good. If he's not there I won't be able to run anyway."

Jake figured that was the truth. He shook his head. "I won't tell."

Chapter Six

Jake started to walk home. He knew he would have to call Dave. But he didn't want to. He really didn't want to.

The street was busier now. The neighborhood had woken up, but Jake felt like he was in a fog. A door slammed in the distance. Jake heard heavy footsteps coming up behind him. He turned.

Simon Patterson ran past, stopped and backed up a few steps.

"Jake?" Behind thick lenses his eyes were round with surprise. "What's up? Everything okay?"

Jake shrugged. "Just out for a run."

"All the way out here? Didn't Dave tell you guys just to do a light run today if you went out at all? Cheese curds, you guys are hard-core. What's a long run for you, to Alaska and back?"

Jake smiled. He was glad Dave had asked Simon to come along to the big race. Then he remembered there wasn't going to be a big race. Unless…Simon wasn't actually running in the race. Could he ask Simon to stay home so there would be an extra seat in the van for Spencer's dad? Jake took a deep breath. He didn't know how to do it without breaking his promise to Spencer or hurting Simon's feelings.

"I've already got my stuff packed," Simon was saying. "Just need snacks and a sleeping bag. I can't wait!"

Jake looked at his curly-haired friend. He opened his mouth but then closed it again. He couldn't find the words after all. He didn't want to go without Simon. But that meant none of them were going to Barry's Bay. A hard lump formed in his throat. Should he break the news to Simon, or should he let Dave do it?

Before Jake could decide, a school bus passed them. Simon took off running. "Gotta go, Jake. That's my bus. See you tomorrow!"

Jake watched until Simon had disappeared inside the bus, then turned around and started walking again. He was going to be late for school, but he couldn't find the energy to run. He needed to call Dave. He needed to think of something else to do this weekend.

A green Jetta pulled over to the curb. Jake's dad hollered to him through the open window. "Jake-o! It's getting late. Want a ride?"

Jake got into the passenger seat and put on his seat belt.

"You've come a long way out this morning. I thought I'd zip you back to the house so you won't be late for school."

Jake nodded. "Thanks. Sometimes running helps me think."

"You must be pretty down about the race, huh?"

Jake didn't answer. He could hardly speak with the lump in his throat.

"It's too bad," said his dad as he put the car in gear and pulled back onto the road. "I was thinking about coming up to Barry's Bay too. I know it's a few hours away, but I thought the race might be pretty exciting to watch."

Jake looked at his father. "Really? What about work?"

"I already had the day booked off. I've been meaning to get that garage cleaned out and some things put away before winter's here—the lawn mower, the patio set, you know—but as soon as you guys qualified I started thinking the garage can wait. It's a pretty big deal, Jake. Your mom and I are so proud of you. And, truth be told, I would have been okay getting away from all that wailing going on as Luke practices for his concert. A quiet ride would have been just the ticket. It would have been a long drive to go solo, but—"

Jake was getting an idea. "What if you had company?"

"Who? Luke and your mom are busy with his big event. There's no way either of them can go."

Jake tried to keep his voice level. This could totally work! "Spencer's dad was thinking about coming up too, but there's no room in the van. Could he catch a ride with you?"

"Why not? It would be great to have the company."

Jake held his breath. "Wait. There's something you need to know. Spencer's dad, he's, uh, he's in a wheelchair."

"What does that matter? Ken Forbes uses a wheelchair, and during hockey season I pick him up every week to go watch the Junior B games. We can put it in the trunk, can't we?"

"That would be so awesome, Dad."

"So does this mean the race might be on after all? Jakester, that's great!"

"Dad, it's the best thing ever!" Jake reached over and gave his dad a high five. They pulled up in front of the house.

"Okay, why don't you sort it out with Spencer and your coach right now? But make it quick or you'll be late for school. See you after work, Jake. Hot dog!"

Chapter Seven

Jake's fingers tingled as he punched in Spencer's number. Would this plan work? It had to. He prayed Spencer was still home.

"Hello?"

"Spencer? It's Jake. Listen. What if my dad picks up your dad and they drive up to Barry's Bay together in his car?"

Spencer was quiet. When he finally answered, his voice was low. "I thought you weren't going to tell anyone what I said."

"This was all my dad's idea. He wants to come see the race, but he doesn't want to drive alone. Your dad would be doing him a big favor."

There was no response.

"Spencer?"

"I'm thinking."

"Okay." Jake was having a hard time being patient, but he knew he had to be.

"Does he know…?"

"He knows and says it's no problem. There's lots of room in the trunk for the chair."

"Can I call you right back?"

Jake looked up at the clock. He had to get to school. "Sure. Take all the time you need."

It seemed like a century passed before the phone rang.

"Jake?"

Jake tried to make his voice sound normal. "Yeah?"

"My dad will come with your dad. He said he'd like to talk to him tonight, to work out the details. Is that okay?"

Jake couldn't speak at first.

"Jake?"

"That's better than good, Spencer. That's great! See you tomorrow."

"Bright and early, I guess."

"Bright and early it is."

"And Jake?"

"Yeah?"

"Thanks."

"No, thank *you*. You're doing us a favor, remember? Tell your dad he can call tonight."

Jake did a crazy little happy dance across the kitchen. Then he ran to grab his backpack. He was on his way out the door when he remembered something. Coach! He scooped up the phone again.

"Dave Driscoll."

"We're on!"

"Who…Jake, is that you?"

"Everybody's good to go, Coach. We'll meet you at your house tomorrow morning as planned."

"But what…how…I thought Spencer couldn't go."

"He worked it out."

"He did? But—"

"And is it okay if my dad and Spencer's dad come up too?"

"Of course. The more, the merrier! But I don't know if we can get another room on such short notice."

A room. Yikes, Jake hadn't thought of that. Everything up there was probably booked. "There are two rooms booked for the team, right? Maybe our dads could have one of those? Us guys can all bunk together. Team spirit, you know."

"You sure?"

"One hundred percent." Jake hoped the guys wouldn't mind.

"Okay, I'll throw some extra foam mats in the van. I'm so glad it worked out. This is great! Amazing. Hey. Aren't you supposed to be in school?"

"On my way. See you in the morning!" They were going to Barry's Bay. Problem solved.

They left at 6:00 AM. Dave's van was packed tighter than a can of Pillsbury dough. Sleeping bags, mats, duffel bags, running spikes, a first-aid kit, a cooler, the tent they stowed their gear in during a race, a case of water and a jumbo box of granola bars. On top of it all sat a box of donuts from their sponsor, Ben's Bakery.

Tall, lanky Shawn sat up front with Dave, his long, skinny legs stretched out in front of him. He pulled out his portable game device and took turns playing with Tony and Spencer, who sat in the seat behind him. Sam finished one Sudoku, then another. Jake read his latest running magazine. They had barely been on the road fifteen minutes when Simon fell fast asleep. As Simon gently snored behind him, Tony laughed. "Some assistant coach."

Dave smiled. "Let him sleep. He's not on duty yet."

The boys started asking questions about the competition, and Dave said what he always said. "It will just be a bunch of guys out there doing their best. I know we can count on you fellows to do the same."

After a while Simon woke up, when Dave turned on the radio. "*Make your party pop*," a perky voice told them, "*with Perry's perfect pizza. Dozens of locations to serve you*."

"Can we stop for pizza?" asked Tony. "I'm starving."

"Why don't you dig out the subs I packed?" asked Dave. "We need to keep going if we're going to get up there in good time. But maybe we'll do pizza tomorrow. We might even have a good reason for a party then, right, guys?" He looked at them in his rearview mirror and winked.

"Pizza, pizza, pizza," the boys chanted. "Party, party, party."

They threw up their hands and high-fived each other over and between the seats. Jake grinned as he settled back into his spot. He liked being with these guys. They were fun. And Spencer was fitting in like an extra squeeze of filling in one of Ben's donuts, making a good thing even better. Everything was awesome.

Chapter Eight

The team was an hour out of Barry's Bay when they heard the Perry's commercial for what seemed like the thousandth time. "Turn it off!" cried Tony. "I can't take it anymore."

"Wait," said Spencer. "Listen." The radio announcer gave the weather forecast. He was calling for snow.

"For real?" asked Shawn. "How close to the North Pole is this place?"

Dave grinned. "Hope you packed your long johns like I told you."

All the boys flattened their faces against the windows to look at the clouds, but Jake saw the look on Spencer's face. He knew he was worried. He scrambled to change the subject. "Anyone for a donut?"

"Pass me one," said Dave.

Jake reached into the back and handed the box around.

"Do you really think it will snow?" asked Spencer.

"Nah," Jake said.

"I don't know, man," said Shawn. "Maybe it'll be a blizzard. Maybe we'll be snowed in for a week."

"No school? Awesome!" said Tony. "As long as there's pizza."

Everyone laughed. Everyone except Spencer. Jake noticed he didn't take a donut either.

"Well, if it's going to look like Christmas, it might as well sound like Christmas," said Shawn. He started singing "Jingle Bells." At the top of his voice. He was not a very good singer. Tony plugged his ears. Simon put his hat on and pulled it down low. Spencer looked ill, but Jake didn't think it was because of the singing. He knew he had to steer the talk away from the weather.

"Hey," he called. "*Would you rather* listen to Shawn sing or play a game?"

"Game!" said Sam. "And that one's my favorite. I've got a good one. Would you rather be thrown into a pit full of snakes or one with spiders?"

Shawn stopped singing. "Snakes!" He shivered. "I hate spiders."

"But spiders—" started Sam.

"Don't even talk about them!" insisted Shawn. "Would you rather surf wearing a parka or ski wearing your swim shorts?"

That kept them going for a while. But eventually the boys ran out of questions and started looking out the windows again. The highway had given way to small curving roads. Everyone grew quiet, staring out at the beautiful scenery. Except for Spencer, who was watching the sky.

They arrived in Barry's Bay and drove right past a couple of hotels.

"Which one is ours?" asked Shawn.

"We check in a little later," said Dave. "I want to check out the course before it gets dark. Make sure you have coats and hats and gloves. It's cold out there."

Lots of other teams must have had the same idea. The parking lot where the race would start was almost full. Teams and coaches huddled everywhere. A group of girls walked by, and one of the runners, tall with brown hair in two long braids, flashed a brilliant smile in the Diamonds' direction.

"She was looking at you, dude," teased Shawn, punching Simon's shoulder.

"Was not."

"Was too, and now you look like a pink puffer fish."

"Do not."

"Your cheeks are on fire."

"It's just from the cold."

The rest of the boys grinned.

"All right," said Dave, pulling a map out of his parka pocket. "Let's do a walk-through of the course." The boys followed him across the parking lot into a wide clearing next to a lake. "This is the start, right here. Everyone's going to run across this field, then head down this path." He led them into the woods. The path started out wide, then narrowed to a boardwalk across a swampy section. The boys followed the trail higher and higher until it finally broke out in a rocky clearing. The team stopped at the top. They could see the whole valley from there.

"Beautiful, isn't it?" said Dave.

"Wow!"

"Awesome!"

"Take it all in while you can, boys. Tomorrow there won't be time to stop."

They took turns doing Tarzan calls and listening for the echo. Spencer was quiet. "What do you think?" Jake asked him. "Is this a great place to run or what?"

"Yeah," said Spencer. "Great."

"Most of the path is really narrow. We're going to have to pass whenever we have a chance."

"Yeah." Spencer's voice was flat.

"You know, I bet our dads will be here by the time we get to the hotel."

"Think so?" His eyes brightened.

Jake looked at his watch. "Yeah, for sure."

"Let's go," called Dave. "We're only halfway through the course, and my nose is turning into an ice cube."

They crossed the clearing and followed the trail down as it curved around giant boulders and scraggly trees. Finally the trees began to thin and the trail began to widen again. Dave pointed out a side trail into a grassy area full of runners and coaches. There was a small shelter and some picnic tables. "This is where the finish will be. Don't miss the turn. Stay tight along the tape, and don't stop until you cross the line."

Chapter Nine

When they pulled into the hotel, Spencer quickly scanned the parking lot. "Jake, what does your dad drive?"

Jake looked around. There were lots of vehicles but no green Jetta. Uh-oh. "Don't worry, Spencer. I'm sure they'll be here soon."

The boys took their bags up to their room and took a look around. Only a few minutes later there was a knock on the door. "Hungry?" Dave asked when Shawn opened the door.

"Starving!" the team cried.

"Okay, then, let's go get some grub."

Most of the boys raced out immediately, but Spencer sat on one of the two single beds.

"Spencer," said Jake.

"Huh?"

"C'mon. Aren't you hungry?"

"Not really." But he got up and followed Jake out of the room.

"Jake," said Dave when they got to the van, "your dad called. He said he and Spencer's dad left later than planned. They're on their way, but they'll be a bit yet. Okay?"

Spencer let out a long, slow breath and nodded. "Okay. Good."

There was a table for six in the center of the restaurant Dave had chosen.

They pulled another chair over and wedged it in.

"Everyone good?" asked Dave as they crowded around.

"It's warm," said Sam.

"And there's food," said Tony.

Even Spencer smiled.

"I still can't believe Dave only got us one room!" said Shawn as he fumbled with the key card. He finally got the door open, and Jake, Sam, Simon and Spencer tumbled in behind him. Tony was helping Dave bring in the foam mattresses.

"Probably a team bonding thing," said Sam.

"It'll be fun," said Jake. He didn't want to tell them it had been his idea.

Sam quickly found the hotel's Wi-Fi password and got his device working. Shawn started skimming through the TV channels.

Suddenly the door was thrown open. "It's snowing!" cried Tony, running to the window and pulling back the curtain. Dave followed him in. "Just started. Look."

They all pressed their noses to the glass. The streetlights lit up the thick flakes, which were falling fast.

"I should have brought my snowboard," said Shawn. "I bet they have some sick hills here."

"Want to go out for a snowball fight?" asked Simon.

"I wonder what it will do to the course," said Sam.

Spencer backed away.

"Spencer, you okay, dude?" asked Shawn.

All eyes turned toward Spencer. He made an attempt at a smile.

"Fine."

"You look like you're about to up-chuck your lasagna," said Tony.

"It's just been a long day," said Jake. "A big trip and a big race tomorrow."

"Yes," said Coach Dave, "but we run for fun, right?" He clapped Spencer on the shoulder and looked at his watch. "Listen, I've got to head to a meeting about the final race details. You guys take it easy. Save the snowboarding and snowballing for after the run so you don't sprain any ankles. Watch some TV maybe, but make sure you're snoring by about nine thirty. Okay?"

"Yes, Coach."

"Simon, I'm counting on you to keep these guys in good shape."

"I'll do my best."

Chapter Ten

A weather alert showed up in a wide red bar along the bottom of the TV screen. Jake moved in front of it and tossed Spencer a sleeping mat. "Why don't we set up our mats?" he said, grabbing the remote and quickly turning the TV off.

"I call one of the beds," called Shawn.

"You're too tall," said Sam. "Your feet will stick out."

"There's no way I'm sleeping on the floor. There might be spiders."

"What's with you and spiders?" asked Simon.

"I don't know. They just have too many legs. It's creepy."

"It makes no sense," said Sam.

"Sure it does. Bugs have six. Spiders have eight. Too many. And sometimes they're hairy. That's just weird."

"Not that part. The being-afraid-of-them part. It makes no sense. They're so tiny."

"Yeah, but still creepy." Shawn lay down on one of the beds. His feet stuck over the end. "I'll bet everyone here is afraid of something."

"No way," said Jake.

"Not me," said Simon.

"Grapes," said Tony.

"What?"

"Grapes. I almost choked on one once. My uncle had to give me the Heimlich. Scariest thing."

"Okay. What about you, Sam? What are you scared of?"

Sam thought for a moment. He sighed. "Well, I guess sometimes I'm afraid of letting people down."

"Whoa. I thought maybe you'd say you were scared of the dark or something," said Shawn. "What do you mean?"

Sam shrugged. "My family, my friends."

"Sam Jii, with all your medals and awards and smarts?"

Sam nodded. "A little. Sometimes."

"C'mon, dude, you're solid. We all know you always do your best." He got up to give Sam a high five, and all the others did the same.

Shawn turned to look at Jake. "How about you, Jake? Feeling good about tomorrow?"

"Don't worry about me. I plan to stick to Spencer like glue and let him take us both right over the finish line. Easy peasy. Right, Spencer?"

Spencer was staring out the window. The snow was still coming down hard.

"Anyone else feel a draft?" asked Jake as he got up and closed the curtains.

"What about you, Spencer?" asked Shawn. "What are you afraid of?"

Jake knew Spencer was waiting for his dad to arrive and was worried about the snow. Jake had promised not to say anything, but he was hoping Spencer would tell the others what was on his mind. They would understand. They would help him out.

"Uh, I don't know...maybe the dentist?"

"You're a dentophobe?" asked Sam.

"Someone who doesn't like the dentist is called a dentophobe?" asked Shawn.

"Yes. And someone who doesn't like water is called an aquaphobe. Ever heard of claustrophobia?"

Simon laughed. "What's that, a fear of Santa Claus?"

"No, it's a fear of small spaces."

"Oh yeah. I knew that," said Shawn. "But when I was little, that dude in the red suit sure freaked me out."

"How about agrizoophobia?" Sam was loving this.

"Are you serious? You made that one up," said Jake.

"No, it's the fear of wild animals."

"Ha! I'm feeling agrizoophobic being caged in here with you guys!" said Shawn.

"Especially if any of you have ablutophobia," added Sam.

"Gross," said Simon. "What's that?"

"A fear of bathing."

"Shouldn't that be called bathophobia?" Simon asked.

Sam shook his head. "Bathmophobia is the fear of stairs."

Shawn threw a pillow at Sam's head. "How do you know all that, man?

"I don't know. I just like collecting weird facts. I think it's fun."

"What's the weirdest one you know?"

"Hmmm. Turophobia maybe? That's the fear of cheese."

"Cheese?" Tony's eyes were wide. "The only thing to be afraid of about cheese is that they'll run out of it when they're making my pizza!"

"I'm not afraid of anything!" declared Simon.

"Oh yeah?"

"Well, maybe that one of you will snore."

"Louder than you do?" They all laughed. Jake yawned. Then so did Shawn. Then Tony.

"Come on, you guys, we'd better get to sleep before Coach Dave pokes his head back in here," said Jake. "Gotta be in tip-top shape for tomorrow, right, Spencer?"

"You guys go ahead. I'm not tired yet."

"You're not a hypnophobe, are you?" asked Sam.

"Let me guess. Afraid of sleep?" asked Spencer. "No, I'm just—"

"What, then?" asked Simon. "Are you really afraid you won't run well tomorrow?" As he spoke he began moving from side to side.

"What are you doing?" asked Jake.

"My job. Assistant coach." Simon started moving his arms up and down like he was swimming the front crawl. "I feel a rap coming on. Here we go."

Silver's rockin', I tell you. Watch out yellow, green and blue.

We've got Shawn who's always on, at the whistle he is gone.

We've got Tony who's no phony, he is strong, that's no baloney.

We've got Sam, Sam I am, he is fast, look out, shazam.

And we've got Jake, he's no fake, when he runs the earth will quake.

And then there's Spencer, he's... intenser.

Makes the others jump the fencer, uhh-hunhh, uhh-hunhh.

As Simon danced, pointed and spun, the others boys burst out laughing.

"Intenser?" asked Sam when he could catch his breath. "That's not even a word."

"That's because Spencer is so awesomely fast, the words to describe him haven't even been invented yet." Simon walked over and punched Spencer on the arm. "Right?"

Spencer smiled and gave him a thumbs-up. Jake saw him pick up the

TV remote. He knew Spencer was probably going to check the weather alerts. He had to think fast. "You know, I think Simon *is* afraid of something," Jake said, grabbing Sam's device. "Give me a second. Yeah, look here. *Venustraphobia.* What do you think, Spencer?" He traded him the device for the remote.

"What is it?" asked Tony.

"Yeah," said Simon, "what is it?"

Spencer cleared his throat. "Venustraphobia. A fear of beautiful women. Symptoms are anxiety, inability to speak, shortness of breath."

"Dude," said Shawn to Simon, "your face is as red as those Spider-Man pajamas! Boys, I think we're onto something."

"I am not afraid of girls!" squeaked Simon, and peals of laughter filled the room again.

"Oh man," said Shawn. "My stomach muscles hurt. I think we'd better try and get some sleep now. I'm going to brush my teeth. No one take my bed." As soon as he closed the bathroom door behind him, there was a bloodcurdling scream.

Tony eyes grew wide. "What—"

"Spider!" Shawn announced, opening the door again. His face was white.

Simon scooped up Sam's device. "Shawn, you...*arachnophobe*. I'm coming to the rescue. I'm not wearing my Spider-Man gear for nothing."

Tony and Sam began rooting around in their bags for toothbrushes too. Jake joined Spencer at the window. "Still snowing?"

Spencer nodded.

"You okay?"

"Sure. But I think I'll wait until our dads are here before I go to sleep."

They heard noises in the hall. "Maybe that's them now," said Jake. He ran over to the door and swung it open.

There stood Coach Dave, all dusted with snow. Jake peered down the empty hallway. "Hey, Coach, everything look good for tomorrow?"

"No worries there. I just stopped in to make sure the party wasn't too wild over here." He winked. "And I got another message from your dads."

Behind him, Jake heard Spencer suck in his breath.

"With all the snow, they decided to stop at a hotel about an hour from here. They will drive up first thing in the morning. The snow's supposed to stop by then."

Jake heard Spencer letting his breath out again slowly. "Okay. Thanks, Dave."

"See you in the morning, team," he called into the room.

"Night, Coach."

The lights were off. Everyone was snuggled deep into their sleeping bags. Jake was just about asleep when he heard someone singing. "The eensy weensy spider went up—"

He heard the thump of Shawn's pillow landing. "Ouch!" said Simon.

Jake smiled and turned over. In the glow of the streetlight he saw a dark shape by the window. Spencer. Jake got up. "Everything okay?" he whispered.

"Yep."

"You know your dad is fine, right?"

"Yes."

"He's one hundred percent safe and sound."

"I know."

"You don't need to worry."

"I'm not."

"You going to be okay for tomorrow?"

"Absolutely."

"Can you sleep?"

"Soon."

Jake sighed. He wished everyone's problems were eensy weensy.

Chapter Eleven

When Jake opened his eyes the next morning, he saw Spencer already up, dressed and sitting in the desk chair. He wore a long-sleeved turtleneck, black leggings with shorts over them, and long socks. His silver jersey hung over the back of the chair along with a winter hat and gloves. He looked ready. But was he?

Jake could see through the crack in the curtains that the snow had stopped and the sun was trying to shine.

There was a knock at the door.

"We don't want any," said Tony from his sleeping-bag cocoon.

Spencer ran to the door and pulled it open.

"Rise and shine, team," Coach Dave said with a grin. "How are you, Spencer? Sleep okay?"

"Yeah, great. Really good."

Spencer's reply surprised Jake. He hoped it was true.

"Excellent." He clapped Spencer on the shoulder. "Because it's race day!"

Jake watched Spencer walk to the window and pull open the curtains for a clear view of the parking lot. He knew the race wasn't the first thing on Spencer's mind.

"Morning, Coach," said Jake, sitting up in his sleeping bag. "Breakfast?"

"You bet. But I'm too old for pajama parties. You guys get up and at 'em. I'll be back in fifteen minutes with supplies, and we'll eat. Last one up has to do the dishes."

Everyone scrambled out of their sleeping bags at once. Jake stretched, quickly dressed and then joined Spencer at the window. "Wow, what a lot of snow!" he said. He immediately knew it was the wrong thing to say. He backtracked. "But look, it's already melting. It's going to be a great day for running, don't you think?"

"It's always a great day for running," said Spencer, but Jake could tell his smile was forced.

Coach Dave returned shortly with a bag of warm bagels, a jar of peanut butter, some plastic knives and a bunch of bananas.

"Hope there's no one here with arachibutyrophobia," said Sam.

Shawn groaned loudly.

"What's the matter?" asked Coach Dave.

"We talked enough about spiders last night."

"Ha!" said Sam with a smile. "That's arachnophobia, remember? *Arachibutyrophobia* is the fear of peanut butter sticking to the roof of your mouth."

"There's a word for that?" said Simon, shaking his head.

"It's all good," said Shawn. "No peanutbutterophobias for me. Pass me that jar."

They sat on the floor in a circle and passed around the fixings for their breakfast.

"I've been thinking, guys," said Simon. He was peeling a banana. "Maybe we can use some of these things to our advantage."

"What do you mean? You're going to throw banana peels along the course and hope the other runners slip?" Sam frowned.

Simon laughed. "No! I mean the phobias we were talking about last night. Tony, you should imagine a big double-cheese pizza at the finish line and run as fast as you can toward it."

They all laughed. "That could work," said Tony.

"I know! Guys, I'm serious. Shawn, imagine an army of spiders behind you. Wouldn't you run faster?"

Shawn shook his head. "No spiders, man."

"What does Spencer need to imagine then?" asked Tony. "The dentist chasing him?"

Spencer smiled. "I'm only here at all because Paul got sick. I figure I'd better run my best for him."

"Yeah, we're like the Musketeers," said Simon, switching gears. "All for one and one for Paul!"

Coach Dave pulled his phone out of his pocket. "I got a text from Paul this morning."

Feeling kind of twitchy, so sick of being itchy. Go, Diamonds!

Laughing, the boys all put their hands into the middle of the circle. "Go, Diamonds!"

The race parking lot was one big puddle. "Careful when you get out," said Dave.

"A green Jetta. That's what you said your dad drives, right?" whispered Spencer.

There was no green Jetta in the lot. "They'll be here soon," answered Jake.

They watched as a car pulled in beside them and two officials got out. One of them pulled a box out of the backseat. It overflowed with medals.

Tony gulped. "Wow, that's a lot of hardware."

"Top three will medal," said Dave as all the boys, eyes wide and mouths hanging slightly open, watched the man walk away with the box. Dave laughed. "But no need to think about that now. Let's focus on the race, not the results."

The boys hopped out of the van.

"I'm setting myself a goal of top fifty," said Shawn.

Dave whistled. "That's a pretty high bar for a race like this."

"Me too," said Tony. "Top fifty."

"Well, go for it! How about the rest of you?"

Spencer was busy scanning the parking lot. Jake was watching Spencer.

"Is it crazy to think I could aim for top ten?" asked Sam. "I really feel like I could do it today."

"Not crazy at all. What you're thinking has a lot to do with how you're running. But let's be smart about it. First things first. Stretches, sprints, snacks.

You know the drill. Simon and I will see if we can find a dry spot to set up the tent."

Sam led the team through a series of stretching exercises. "Okay," he said when they were done. "Let's warm up a bit more with a jog." He and Shawn and Tony took off. Spencer didn't move. Jake waited with him. "You guys coming?" asked Sam, looking over his shoulder.

"Be right there," said Jake. "You guys go ahead." He moved closer to Spencer. "You okay?"

"I don't think I can do this. I mean, I thought I could, but now—"

"You can."

"I wish my dad was here."

"He'll be here."

"Something must have happened. What if he needs me?"

"He's fine."

"You don't know that."

"He's with my dad. We would have heard if something was wrong. Right now *we* need you."

Spencer's face darkened. "So you can win."

"No!" Jake tried not to get angry. "No. So we can run a good race. The best race we can."

Spencer sighed. "I don't know."

"Listen, Spencer," said Jake. "You've got to get in the zone. Your fear about your dad is holding you back big-time. Let it melt away like all this snow is doing. He's on his way. You know he is. What would he want you to do right now?"

Spencer sighed again. "Run."

"Then let's run."

Chapter Twelve

They ran, but Spencer wasn't loosening up. He ran stiffly and kept glancing from side to side instead of concentrating on what was in front of him. Jake was getting more and more uptight, worrying about Spencer worrying. He was beginning to wonder himself where their dads were. They should have been there by now. It was almost time for the race to start.

They found the tent Simon and Dave had set up. Shawn, Tony and Sam were already there, each with a water bottle. "Let's get a drink," said Jake, steering Spencer over. He had just a few minutes left to get Spencer refocused. "Hey, Coach, Spencer's got a question about how to handle the downhill section of the course. Could you go over that again?" Spencer gave Jake a funny look.

"Sure," said Dave. "What do you need to know?"

"And Simon, find Spencer a water bottle, will you? I need to find the restrooms."

Jake walked away. He needed to use the restroom, but he also needed a few minutes to think. Sam was ready. Shawn was ready. Tony was ready to go. They would all do their absolute best.

But Spencer wasn't ready, and that was a shame, because of all of them Spencer Solomon had it in him to win this race. Right now Jake didn't even know if they could get him to run it. He had tried to distract him, but that had not been enough. Now he needed to inspire him. But how? He needed more than the promise of pizza.

On his way back from the restroom Jake still hadn't come up with an idea. He wasn't sure what else he could do. If he didn't—

"Jake!"

Jake looked over. "Dad! Mr. Solomon! You're here!"

"You haven't run yet, have you?"

Jake shook his head.

"We were beginning to think we were going to miss everything. The road was blocked by a tractor-trailer that must have gone over in the snow yesterday.

It was finally cleared, so now here we are. We tried to call Dave, but with all the hills and valleys around here, there was no reception."

"We're just about to get started. Spencer will be so glad to see you!"

"Probably better if we head for the finish," said Spencer's dad. "I think it will be easier for me to set up over there. This beat-up old chair fit nicely in the trunk, but the wheels aren't the greatest. I left my fancy electric one at home. I'm afraid it's going to take some pushing, Ed."

"No problem," said Jake's dad. "Just point us in the right direction, Jake."

Jake showed them the course map that was tacked to the outside wall of the restrooms. "The finish line is here," he said. "Want me to show you how to get there?"

"No, you get going," said Mr. Solomon. "We don't want you to miss your race. Tell Spencer I'll see him at the finish. How's he doing?"

"Great!" At least, he will be now, thought Jake. He turned to go, then looked back quickly. "I'm really glad you're here, Dad. You too, Mr. Solomon."

His dad grinned and gave him the thumbs-up sign. "So are we. Give it all you've got, Jake-o."

Jake sprinted to the starting area. "Spencer!"

"Jake, it's no use. I can't do this. I feel awful. My stomach's all knotted up. My head hurts. I don't know what to do."

"I saw your dad. He's here! He's good. Everything's good."

Spencer looked around. "Where? Where is he?"

"They've gone to the finish."

"I'm going to see."

"No. There's no time. Look, we're ready to start." A tall man walked into the center of the clearing, blew sharply on his whistle and shouted to the teams to line up. An eager runner knocked into the official on his way to the line and made him drop his whistle. It disappeared in a patch of snow. The official scowled.

"You know, that's not a whistle anymore," said Simon as he watched the official lift it out of the snow, shake it off and try to use it again. It sounded like someone letting the air out of a balloon.

Shawn had a puzzled look on his face. "What is it then?"

"Snow blower," Simon said with a grin.

Spencer pulled Jake aside. "I need to see my dad."

"You will. At the finish."

Spencer crossed his arms. "I don't believe you. He's not really here. You're just saying that because you want me to run."

Jake reached out and put his hand on Spencer's shoulder. Spencer shook it off. Jake took a deep breath. "I do. I do want you to run. But Spencer, you have to believe me. I'm not lying. Your dad is here."

"He would have come and seen me."

"He said to tell you he *will* see you. At the finish. My dad and your dad are working their way over there right now. They'll be there. Trust me."

Spencer looked at Jake, then looked away.

The whistle sounded once more. "Here we go, fellas," called Dave. "Time for takeoff." Shawn and Tony moved in behind Sam. Jake began moving forward, but Spencer positioned himself at the end of the line. Jake stopped. Dave raised an eyebrow. "What's up? That's not how we planned it."

Jake thought about it. Spencer had the best time. He was supposed to be their first runner out. Was Spencer hanging back because his heart wasn't in the race? Was he thinking of cutting out to go look for his dad? Or was he just angry with Jake and didn't want to stand next to him? Jake wanted to explain everything to the team so they'd understand. But there wasn't time, and he had promised Spencer he'd keep quiet. But he had to say something. "We've been talking, Coach. We think this lineup will work better. I, uh, I don't really have time to explain why, but we've got it figured out."

Dave looked at the others. "You guys okay with this?" Jake made eye contact with each of his teammates, silently pleading with them to go along. They seemed to get the message.

"Sure," said Tony.

"Works for me," said Shawn.

"Go, Diamonds," said Sam.

"Last call, all teams," shouted the tall official. Just then another man ran over to talk to him. The tall man put his hands on his hips and listened intently. Then he blew a long blast on his whistle, just like a referee would to signal the end of a soccer match. "Your attention, please. The race will be delayed by ten minutes while we locate the starting pistol. Race delay, ten minutes."

Dave shook his head. "I've never seen that happen before. At ease, team. Stay loose."

Chapter Thirteen

Jake grabbed Spencer by the elbow and hauled him away from the others. "I need to know if you're in," he demanded.

"I'm in."

Jake felt a rush of relief.

"I really want out, but I'm in. I want to go over and find my dad but I can't let the team down. Or Paul. I'll do my best, but let me be the last runner out. I don't want to slow anyone down."

"Okay, but Spencer…"

"Just give me a minute, okay?" Spencer's voice cracked. Jake could tell he was having a hard time keeping things together.

Another runner came close to where Spencer and Jake were standing. He wore black gloves and a black hat, and there was a Ravens logo on his black shirt. He looked Spencer up and down. He was a full head taller than Spencer was and wide as a refrigerator box. "What's the matter, little man?" he asked. "Scared? Can't take the pressure of the big race?"

"Back off," said Jake.

The Ravens runner hooked Jake's jersey with a gloved finger. "Diamonds, huh? Psssht. Wimps."

"Look, you don't understand—"

"Sure I do. You think you've got what it takes to travel a tough race like this? We'll just see how it ends." He let go of Jake's shirt and walked back to his team.

"Take your minute," said Jake. Spencer nodded. Jake walked back toward the others. "Dave," he called, "I'm going to run over to the restroom one more time."

"Now?"

"Nerves. You know. Be right back."

"But there's no time."

"I'll be back. Trust me!"

Dave threw his hands up in the air. "This is the craziest race I've ever been to."

Jake jogged away, but he didn't go to the restrooms. He waited just out of sight at the edge of the clearing. He saw the official return to his place ahead of the starting line, heard the whistle blow, saw the teams move into position. He saw his teammates line up, Sam, Shawn, Tony, and felt a stab of joy when he saw Spencer join them. He watched Simon high-five each of them, wishing them a good race. He saw Dave scanning the runners, searching for him. He ran in just as the official raised the gun.

Dave let out his breath. Spencer backed up to make space for Jake in the lineup.

"I'm good back here," said Jake. Spencer turned and gave him a look. They both jumped at the sound of the gun. All the runners surged forward. "Go!" Jake shouted.

It was chaos. A runner in green shot forward, and hundreds of feet churned after him through the mud and the slush to the end of the field. Jake loved this part. He wanted to work his way through the crowd so he could be in a good position heading into the woods, but he forced himself to stick to Spencer like a shadow. He was surrounded by a sea of jerseys. Yellow, green, orange, blue, red. Suddenly a black cloud descended as the burly Raven they'd met earlier crossed into their path. He continued to push left until his feet nearly tangled with Spencer's. Had he done that on purpose? Was he trying to trip Spencer? Get a grip, thought Jake. There are an awful lot of feet out here.

They reached the end of the clearing, slowing as runners jostled to find a place on the trail. Spencer glanced back over his shoulder. Jake was right behind him. "There's a spot up ahead where you can pass, Jake."

"No."

"Yes, there is. I remember it."

"I'm not going to pass."

"I still don't feel so good. I can't get a rhythm going. I—"

"I am not going to pass you. I'm going to stay behind you all the way."

"What?"

"You heard me. Your dad is here, Spencer. He will meet you at the finish. The sooner you get there, the sooner you'll know I'm telling the truth. I'm going to make sure you get across that line. I am not going to pass, so you'd better get going."

Spencer threw another quick look over his shoulder.

Jake pulled a face. "I told the guys I was going to stick to you like glue, remember? This is all you're going to see back here for the entire race, so you might want to look ahead instead."

Spencer barked out a laugh. Then he shook out his fingers, rolled his shoulders back and began to run faster.

They reached the boardwalk, and Spencer began to get a rhythm. His breathing started to become more even. Good, thought Jake. Good. Jake kept his eyes trained on Spencer's silver jersey in front of him.

He and Spencer slipped in the mud and soggy leaves at times, but they kept moving steadily forward. Up ahead the path would turn and become steeper. There was a big rock next to the trail, marking the spot. Jake smiled when he spotted Coach Dave perched on top of it. "That's it, boys," he called. "Pace it out now. Up you go. Just run."

Spencer made the turn and took off. *Yes!* This was more like it. Jake found a higher gear, the muscles in his calves burning with the uphill climb. His lower back began to ache, but he didn't pay any attention. He was focused on following that silver jersey.

Many runners began to slow, but not Spencer. He flew through the trees. They began to pass groups of runners where the trail widened and slid past runners one by one when it was narrow. That's it, thought Jake, following and fighting to keep his breathing even. He jumped roots and stones, splashed through slush, ducked under low-hanging branches, batted away spiderwebs and tried to ignore the cold water seeping into his shoes.

"Still there?" Spencer called over his shoulder.

"Like glue." It was getting harder, but Jake was determined to keep up. They hadn't made the halfway point yet. Still a long way to go. But Jake knew Spencer was no longer just back in the race. He was back on track to win. That idea was giving Jake a whole new kind of energy.

Chapter Fourteen

They burst through the last of the trees and came out at the top of the cliff. Finally. The high point of the trail. Halfway. The wind bit at Jake's nose. He narrowed his eyes to a squint. His legs felt like logs, and his throat burned. He didn't know if he could keep going at this pace.

"Well done! Looking strong! And it's all downhill from here!"

Jake didn't know how Coach Dave managed to pop up along the trail the way he did, but his words gave Jake just the boost he needed. Half a dozen runners ahead of them were almost across the rocky clearing and were making their way back to the trees and the downward trail. Spencer pointed, and Jake knew he meant they had to get in front of this group before the path narrowed again and they got caught with no place to pass. They began to sprint. Yellow shirt. Orange. Navy. Red. Silver. Sam. He grinned as Spencer and Jake shot past him. "Go, Diamonds!" he shouted.

Ahead, a lone runner disappeared into the darkness of the trees. Black jersey. When he heard feet pounding on the path behind him, the big Raven glanced over his shoulder and looked at them darkly. "Go, Diamonds," he called out in a falsetto voice. "Wimps," he added before taking off. Jake wanted to reply but knew it was wiser to save his breath. They still had some serious ground to cover.

It was almost harder running downhill than it had been going up. The trail was muddy, and the loose gravel was slippery. More than once Jake had to grab hold of a branch to help him stay on his feet. Spencer began to pull away, and Jake worked hard to stick close. It was a brutal pace. After hooking his foot on a root, Jake glanced down to make sure his laces were still tied. When he looked up again he saw that Spencer had begun to slow. *Oh no*. What now?

Spencer had caught up to the runner in black. The trail was narrow, and the Raven was holding his arms out at his sides in a T shape so Spencer couldn't pass.

"You know," Spencer said quietly, "you can run faster if you use your arms."

The Ravens runner laughed. "There's three guys up there," he huffed. "One of them's on my team. I won't catch them. But that's okay. I don't need to." He paused to catch his breath but did not lower his arms. "I just need to stay ahead of you two. That way we won't be beat by a couple of sissies."

Three guys? They were that close? Jake tried to get a view of the trail up ahead. It looked like it widened a little. Hope, mixed with the frustration he felt toward the Raven, made him forget how much his lungs hurt and his ankles ached. Somehow they needed to get past this guy. When the trail opened up they'd be ready.

Very soon the trail did get wider, too wide for the bully to block them by holding his arms out. He began to swerve from side to side to prevent them from getting by. Jake was growing angry. He wished Coach Dave would pop up along the path right now. He forced himself right up on Spencer's heels. "There's only one way to beat this guy," he panted in a low voice so the black-shirted runner couldn't hear.

"What's that?"

"Together. We both go at once. He can't block both sides at the same time."

Spencer nodded. "Ready?"

"When you are."

Spencer took a deep breath. "Now."

They both raced up behind the Raven. When he swerved left, Jake snuck by on his right. He watched over his shoulder to see Spencer come through. Reflex made the bully swing to the right, and Spencer sped up to surge past on the left. But he didn't quite make it. The Raven drove back to the left, grabbed the back of Spencer's jersey and hauled him down. Jake skidded to a stop. The bully shoved him hard as he pushed his way past.

"You can't do that!" Jake shouted.

"Do what?" the Raven called back.

Jake watched helplessly as the black shirt disappeared around a turn in the trail. He ran to Spencer. He had scraped both hands on the gravel and clocked his chin on a rock in the path.

"Spencer! Are you okay?"

"Jake, what are you doing? You were past him. Get out of here. Get going. We're almost at the finish."

"I can't leave you here."

"I'm fine. I'm coming. I just need a second. I'll be right behind you. Trust me."

"I'm not leaving. We have to do something. That guy can't just—"

"Jake, you really want to do something? Go catch that guy. I will be right behind you. I promise." Jake heard a noise in the woods. Runners? He wished with all his heart it was Dave. He tried to peer through the trees. Was that a flash of orange?

"Jake! This is a race!" Spencer was on his feet now. Blood was dripping from the cut on his chin. He wiped it with his glove. He looked at Jake and nodded. "Go."

Jake went. Anger made his throat feel tight and balled his hands up into fists. But it was only partly rage at what the bully had done that helped propel him down that path. It was what Spencer had said that gave Jake the real fuel for a fight to the finish. This was a race. Time to lay it all down. Time to just run.

Chapter Fifteen

The trail leveled out and the trees began to thin. At every turn Jake hoped to catch a glimpse of the Ravens runner, but so far he hadn't seen a soul. He didn't hear anyone behind him either. Was Spencer all right? It made Jake's chest ache to think of Spencer not flying across that finish line the way only he could. It just wasn't fair.

Jake tried hard to focus. He watched for rocks or roots that might trip him up. Part of him was afraid Spencer wasn't coming up from behind. Another part of him was afraid the boy in black was hiding somewhere, waiting to jump out at him when he least expected it. Jake forced himself to concentrate on running, counting in his head so that he stuck to a regular, punishing pace.

When Jake did hear footsteps crunching on the gravel behind him, fear crawled up his spine like a snake in his shirt. He debated whether he should speed up and try to outrun the bigger boy or turn and face him. He didn't know if he had it in him to go any faster. Jake closed his eyes, then opened them just enough to peer quickly over his shoulder. What he saw made his knees go soft. Spencer! He almost drowned in a wave of relief.

Spencer pulled up to him.

"You okay?" Jake asked.

Spencer nodded. "There's only one way to do this."

"What's that?"

"Together."

Legs churning, arms pumping, they flew down the path side by side. One hundred yards ahead Jake could see the flags marking the turn into the clearing and the tape stretching along the field to the finish. He saw something else as well. The Ravens runner wasn't far from the turn.

Jake's leg muscles were straining, stretching, screaming. Blood was pounding in his ears as he thundered around the turn beside Spencer. The huge breaths of cold air he pulled in did little to cool the fire in his chest. They were closing in on the black shirt ahead of them, but the finish line was in sight. People along the tape were yelling, clapping their mittened hands.

Dig. Dig. Run. Jake's vision started to blur, but there was no stopping now. The three runners barreled toward the orange pylons that marked the finish. In a flurry of pumping fists and feet they flew across it. The Raven, Spencer and then Jake, barely a step behind.

Simon was at the line. He high-fived Spencer and Jake so hard he nearly knocked them to the ground. Dave was there too, his eyes as big as medals. "That was unbelievable. I can't believe that finish. Full tilt. You guys okay?"

Jake couldn't speak. He was pointing ahead of him and scanning the crowd for the Raven.

"Where is he?" asked Spencer, breathing heavily.

Yes, thought Jake, nodding. The runner in black. They needed to tell Dave what had happened. But he still couldn't speak. He couldn't get enough air. His knees wanted to fold. He closed his eyes. He needed to sit down.

"Is my dad here?"

Of course. That was who Spencer was looking for.

Dave grinned. "Your fans are right over here. I'll show you." Spencer followed Dave. Jake stumbled after them.

"Spencer!" a voice called from the crowd.

Spencer ran. How could he still run? "Dad. You're here!"

"You bet. Front-row seats. Not bad, eh?"

"You're okay?"

"We've been having a fine time. You weren't worried, were you?"

"No…I'm…it's good to see you."

Spencer's dad grabbed him in a bear hug. "It's good to see you too. That was amazing."

Jake squeezed his way through the crowd and stood panting, hands on his knees. His dad caught him in a headlock and messed up his hair. "Jake! That was some race."

"Incredible," said Mr. Solomon. "Fifth and sixth. In a provincial race. It's a good thing I saw it with my own eyes or I might not believe it." He grinned. "You must have been running full out the whole time."

"Ah, we had a bit of a rough start."

"Oh?"

"And some trouble partway through."

"Well, you sure put in a great finish."

"It's not over yet," shouted Simon. "Here comes Sam."

A runner in a purple jersey crossed the line. Then one in white. Behind them, Sam was battling it out with three others, one in orange, one in black, one in red. "All the way, Sam," they yelled. "Go, Diamonds!"

Orange was ahead. Then red. Then silver. They pounded down along the tape. Ten yards to go. Five. Two. Orange was first, but what happened after that was a blur. "Pretty sure Sam was next. Almost positive. That would make him top ten," crowed Simon. "Top ten! I thought he was nuts when he said he'd shoot for top ten! Man, this is exciting. You guys are leaving them in the Diamonds dust." He scooped up a bottle of water and ran to find Sam.

Jake's dad put a hand on his son's shoulder. "You okay?"

"Getting there." Jake's voice was shaky. His knees were shaky. "It was quite a run."

"I'll bet. Take it easy then. Who are we looking for now?"

"Shawn." He scanned the field. "And Tony." They watched runners come in singly or in groups of two or three. No sign of the remaining Diamonds yet.

Mr. Solomon was telling Spencer all about the dads' trip up to Barry's Bay. He was grinning, and his eyes were bright.

"So it was a good trip then? Even with the snow and everything?" Spencer asked.

"It was excellent. We stopped before the snow got too bad. Just took our time. I'm glad you could come up with your team and focus completely on the race. You did so well, Spence. I'm glad."

Spencer looked out at the course. He shook his head. His hand was resting on the back of his dad's wheelchair. He turned to look at Jake's dad. "Thanks for making the trip up here, Mr. Jarvis."

"My pleasure. I wouldn't miss this for anything. Beats cleaning out the garage. About time we saw some more silver shirts coming home, you think?"

"Should be soon," said Jake.

Spencer grinned suddenly. "Good thing we cleared out all the spiderwebs from across that trail, hey, Jake? Before Shawn came through?"

His dad looked up at him. "Spiderwebs? What—hey, that's quite a scuff you've got on your chin. Do you need something for that? What happened? Does it hurt?"

Spencer touched his chin carefully with his fingers. "I think the blood is pretty well dried up. Long story." He glanced over at Jake. "We'll tell you about it later. Here comes Shawn."

"Which one?"

"The tall one. With all the hair."

"Shawn! Bring it on! Dig, dude, dig!"

"Hot dog! I bet he's going to finish mid-forties," said Jake's dad as Shawn loped across the finish line. "You guys are on fire."

Chapter Sixteen

The crowd kept cheering, looking for more runners battling down the home stretch. Jake moved in beside Spencer. "We've got to tell Coach about what happened out there."

Spencer shrugged.

"That Ravens runner did something dirty. We can't let him get away with it."

"I know, but it's only you and me who know what happened. We're both on the same team. He'll deny it and say I tripped on a root or something and we made up a story. Who's going to believe us?"

Jake thought for a moment. "But it's not fair."

"No, it isn't. But I know what happened, and you know what happened. We almost got him." Spencer looked at Jake. Then he looked down. "Hey, what's this?" He pulled a pizza box from a pocket behind the seat of his dad's wheelchair. "You guys went to Perry's?"

"Last night," said Jake's dad. "Delicious. You guys should try it."

"I forgot that box was still in there," said Spencer's dad. "We ate the leftovers for breakfast."

"You don't let me eat pizza for breakfast."

"Special occasion."

"This is just what we need," said Jake. "Tell me when you see Tony make the turn."

Another orange runner came in. Then white and navy blue.

"Come on, Tony," murmured Jake. "Top fifty. It must be getting close."

Simon, Sam, Shawn and Dave all moved in behind them at the tape. Jake and Spencer high-fived their teammates and introduced their dads.

"You okay?" asked Jake.

"A little wobbly," said Shawn. "I came in number forty-three. Had all the burners firing at max. And I only bumped my head on a branch once."

Jake noticed the red mark on his teammate's forehead and winced.

"I guess Sam was in a real big hurry," Shawn continued. "Someone must have told him one of the prizes was a trip to the Space Station. And I hear you two laid down some solid scores. Easy peasy, just like you said, hey, Jake?"

Jake looked over at Spencer. Easy peasy didn't quite describe it.

"Hope Tony makes it in soon. He's the anchor."

They all looked back out at the field.

"What's that?" asked Shawn, pointing to the box in Jake's hands.

"Secret weapon," Jake said with a grin. He showed them the Perry's logo.

"Beauty."

They waited. For a long while there was no one. Then the crowd erupted once more. A red runner came in. Then green. Yellow and purple made the turn together and made a run for the finish.

"There," yelled Simon, pointing.

A runner in a burgundy jersey had just made the turn. Tony was right on his heels. He stumbled a little taking the corner. He was breathing hard, and he looked spent. It was forty yards to the line.

"Oh boy," said Coach Dave, sucking in his breath

"To-ny! To-ny!" his teammates chanted.

Jake waved the Perry's Pizza box high above his head. "Come on, Tony. Come on."

Tony looked up. A big smile split his face, followed by a look of sheer determination. His forehead wrinkled, and his eyes narrowed. Arms pumping, feet pounding, he began to charge ahead, faster, faster, until he stormed across the line inches ahead of the other runner.

"Pizza power!" The boys untangled themselves from the crowd and went to find Tony.

"Be right back," Spencer called to his dad.

"Take your time."

They swarmed Tony where he was standing, breathing hard. "I was one spot short of top fifty. One short. But it doesn't matter because I've got pizza!" He grabbed the box from Jake. His eyes went wide. "Empty?"

Coach Dave jogged up and laughed. "You'll get your pizza, Tony. Don't you worry. You deserve a dozen! A lifetime supply! You guys did a great job out there. I can't believe how you all did. I want to hear all about it, but first you need to do a bit of a cooldown. Tony, you take a walk around. Get some water. You other guys take a slow jog and then grab a snack and find some warmer clothes to put on." He grinned. "That was some race."

"I'm so hungry!" said Tony as the team walked back to the tent after the cooldown. "Where's that big box of granola bars?"

They found Simon sitting in the door of the tent. "Finally!" he said. "I think all the runners are in. Are the results posted yet?"

"I don't know. Let's go check," said Jake, pulling on his jacket.

The boys grabbed their snacks and made their way down to the picnic shelter. The area around the results board was crowded.

Shawn stood on his toes and craned his neck. "I see your name, Spencer. Number four! And Jake, you're fifth. That's all I can see so far."

"Wait. That can't be right," said Spencer.

Jake looked around. "Where's Coach Dave?"

Chapter Seventeen

The Diamonds heard a shout behind them. Coach Dave was walking quickly toward them. His smile was so wide he looked like he was about to split in two.

"Coach, the results—they made a mistake," said Jake.

"No mistake." He shook his head. "I've just had an update on the placings." Dave took a deep breath. "Two runners were disqualified from the race, which is too bad. One of them took a wrong turn near the beginning. They found him, but he didn't finish. But that has nothing to do with your results." He took another deep breath. "The other runner was disqualified for unsportsmanlike behavior. One of the course monitors witnessed a runner from the Ravens tripping another runner and reported it."

Jake held his breath. Someone had seen Spencer go down?

"That's the kind of thing you don't really expect to see at this level of competition. But because that runner was disqualified, everyone who came in after him moves up by one place."

"All of us?" asked Spencer, looking over at Jake. "So we *are* fourth and fifth."

"I'm ninth?" asked Sam.

"Oh, man," said Shawn, "Three Diamonds in the top ten! That is so amazing. But a little bit brutal too. Just out of the medals. *Just.* So close, dudes."

"Well, that's not actually true." The coach could hardly contain himself.

"What?" Everyone said the word at the same time.

"It looks like all of you will be picking up some hardware before we leave."

"Hold on. You said there were medals for the top three finishers," said Jake.

"Yes, the top three individuals. *And* the top three teams. The Diamonds came in…are you ready for this?" Coach Dave did a weird little happy dance."First!"

"*What*?" the boys all said again.

"First!"

"But how?" asked Spencer. "We heard that some guy in green was way, way ahead, like in another time zone."

"Yeah, wasn't he something? Such a great runner. He'll get the first-place individual medal. But after counting up the points based on how each of you finished, the gold team medal goes to you guys."

The boys stared at each other. Then Shawn began to whoop. Sam raised his hands in the air like a prizefighter. Simon flung his arms around Spencer and Jake's shoulders, and the three of them began to jump up and down. Tony just stood and stared.

"Tony," said Shawn. "You okay?"

"I think he's in shock," said Sam.

Tony shook his head. He looked over at Coach Dave. "I just managed to make my way to the front and see the board. I saw Shawn's name at forty-two and mine a few names below it. Everyone moving up by one means I broke top fifty!"

Everyone mobbed Tony. Then the whole team went down in a heap. "Go, Diamonds!"

Jake's dad arrived, pushing Spencer's dad in his wheelchair over the bumpy ground.

"Dad!" Spencer and Jake both yelled at once.

"We know—we heard. Well done!"

After about a hundred high fives, they noticed a man in an orange safety vest standing nearby. He was smiling. "Excuse me for interrupting your celebration, but I wanted to come and congratulate you too. Nice work, Diamonds! First place!" He turned to Spencer. "How are you doing? I saw that other runner knock you down."

Everyone looked at Spencer.

"I tried to get to you. I thought you might be hurt. But then I saw you get back up again, and your friend was with you. I didn't want to slow you down. From what I hear, you almost caught that guy at the finish." He shook

Spencer's hand. Then he turned and shook Jake's too. "That's the spirit, fellas. That was some great running."

"So that's where you got the scrapes on your hands and the gash on your chin?" asked Coach Dave. "Why didn't you say something?"

Spencer shrugged. "I'm okay. Jake was there."

"Well, I'm impressed. Especially considering how you two still came flying across the finish line like twin tornados."

"That's the way to do it," said Mr. Solomon. "Right, Spencer? You might get knocked down, but that doesn't mean you quit." He paused. "I used to run myself. Absolutely loved it."

There was an awkward moment in which no one said a word. Spencer looked down at the dirt. Jake felt his chest go tight.

Mr. Solomon smiled. "But I also loved watching Spencer and the rest of you boys run today. I hope you keep it up for a long time. Being out on the trail with friends like this—there's nothing better. Sometimes the course we're on takes an unexpected turn, but we find a way keep on going."

"Just be sure you duck when you need to," said Shawn, rubbing his forehead. Everyone laughed.

"That was the best pizza I have ever tasted," said Tony as they walked out of Perry's Pizza.

"I'm surprised you tasted anything at all, you were eating so fast," said Shawn.

"I slowed down after the first four slices."

"We sure did make that party pop," said Simon.

"It was cool they gave us sundaes for free," said Sam.

"Hot as lava, cool as ice cream," said Coach Dave. "So, gang? Time to head home?" He slid the door of the van open. Spencer and Jake went over to the Jetta with their dads, but the rest of the team climbed in.

"Hey, did you know that a group of spiders is called a clutter?" asked Sam with a grin.

"No!" said Shawn. "If you don't cut out the spider talk, I'm going to sing all the way home."

"*Would you rather*," said Tony, "listen to Shawn sing one hour every day for the rest of your life or die right now from a poison arrow?"

"Poison arrow!" they all cried.

Spencer helped his dad into the Jetta. Jake folded up the wheelchair and put it in the trunk. His dad gave him a high five and climbed into the driver's seat. "I really enjoyed watching the race, Jake. See you at home."

"You too, Spencer," said Mr. Solomon. "Have a good ride."

"You're sure you don't want me to ride home with you?"

"No, you should go with your friends. Have fun."

"I guess that worked out," said Spencer as the Jetta disappeared from view. "My dad asked if we had any more races coming up. He and your dad are all ready to plan another road trip."

Jake smiled. He looked down at his medal. "You really are a great runner, Spencer. Thanks for coming. We really needed you."

"No, Jake," said Spencer as they made their way over to the van. "I'm pretty sure it was the other way around."

The door slid open again. "Enter if you dare," said Simon.

"If we dare?" Jake looked at Spencer. "We are not afraid!"

"I am," said Coach Dave. "The way you guys eat, I can't afford to buy any more food. Come on, we've got to get Tony home before dinner."

Acknowledgments

Many thanks to all the young readers who asked for this story to be written; to all the runners, coaches and parents who were its inspiration; to the amazing team at Orca Books who worked to bring it to print; and to my family, who always cheer me on.

Sylvia Taekema's first novel, *Seconds*, was voted a Silver Birch Express Award Honour Book. Sylvia enjoys visiting classrooms and libraries and meeting with readers and writers of all ages. She also loves to read, bake cookies and go on camping adventures with her family. She lives in Chatham, Ontario. For more information, visit sylviataekema.wordpress.com.

Titles in the Series

Orca currents

For more information on all the books
in the Orca Currents series, please visit
orcabook.com.